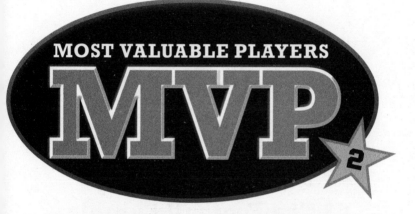

MOST VALUABLE PLAYERS

MVP 2

THE **SOCCER SURPRISE**

MVP

Also by David A. Kelly

The Ballpark Mysteries® series

*Babe Ruth and the
Baseball Curse*

MOST VALUABLE PLAYERS
MVP
2

THE SOCCER SURPRISE

David A. Kelly

illustrated by Scott Brundage

A STEPPING STONE BOOK™

Random House New York

To my editors, Caroline Abbey and Paula Sadler,
who helped create the MVP club. Thank you.
—D.A.K.

Text copyright © 2016 by David A. Kelly

Cover art and interior illustrations copyright © 2016 by Scott Brundage

All rights reserved. Published in the United States by Random House Children's Books, a division of Penguin Random House LLC, New York.
Random House and the colophon are registered trademarks and A Stepping Stone Book and the colophon are trademarks of Penguin Random House LLC.
Ballpark Mysteries® is a registered trademark of Upside Research, Inc.

Visit us on the Web!
SteppingStonesBooks.com
randomhousekids.com

Educators and librarians, for a variety of teaching tools, visit us at RHTeachersLibrarians.com

Library of Congress Cataloging-in-Publication Data
Names: Kelly, David A. (David Andrew), author. | Brundage, Scott, illustrator.
Title: The soccer surprise / David A. Kelly ; illustrated by Scott Brundage.
Description: New York : Random House, [2016] | Series: MVP ; #2 | "A Stepping Stone book." |
Summary: "A famous soccer star is coming to town, but can practice with a pro help the MVP kids score big at their next game?"—Provided by publisher.
Identifiers: LCCN 2015029517 | ISBN 978-0-553-51322-6 (paperback) | ISBN 978-0-553-51323-3 (hardcover library binding) | ISBN 978-0-553-51324-0 (ebook)
Subjects: | CYAC: Soccer—Fiction. | Clubs—Fiction. | Friendship—Fiction. |
BISAC: JUVENILE FICTION / Sports & Recreation / Soccer. | JUVENILE FICTION / Mysteries & Detective Stories. | JUVENILE FICTION / School & Education.
Classification: LCC PZ7.K2936 So 2016 | DDC [Fic]—dc23
LC record available at http://lccn.loc.gov/2015029517

Printed in the United States of America
10 9 8 7 6 5 4 3 2 1

This book has been officially leveled by using the F&P Text Level Gradient™ Leveling System.

Random House Children's Books supports the First Amendment and celebrates the right to read.

CONTENTS

MVP Stats

Meet the MVPs!

MAX

Great athlete—
and a great detective

ALICE

Archery ace
and animal lover

NICO

Can't wait to practice
and can't wait to play

LUKE

Loves to exercise
his funny bone

KAT

Captures the best
game-day moments
on camera

A SMASHING KICK

"Over here!" Kat called as she ran toward the other team's goal. "I can do it!"

There were only seconds left in the soccer game. The Franklin Elementary School girls were playing the boys. The game was tied 1–1.

Kat's best friend Alice lofted a pass to her. Kat trapped the ball with her foot. She turned for the shot and blasted it. Kat's teammates screamed as the ball sliced through the air toward the goal!

But at the last second, the ball hit the post and bounced over the top of the net.

No goal! The gym teacher's whistle blew. Game over. It was a tie.

The boys' team cheered! A tie was better than losing. The girls drifted off the field with shoulders drooped. They would have won if Kat's shot had gone in.

Alice skidded to a stop beside Kat. Alice was athletic and lucky. Even when she missed a shot or messed up a pass, she usually scored the next goal or soon made a nice assist.

"Aw! I was so close!" Kat cried. She

dropped down to the grass and pulled a bright blue hair tie from her hair. Black curls tumbled around her neck.

"Good try," Alice said. "Just a bit to the right and you would have had it."

"I keep missing those shots!" Kat said. "I've got to find a way to get better before the big game in two weeks."

Each year, the girls' team played the Wilton Warriors. Lots of people came to watch and cheer their team on. The Warriors usually won, but Franklin's team had been practicing hard. They really wanted to win this year.

Kat's twin brother, Luke, walked up next to her. He patted her on the shoulder.

"Nice try, sis," Luke said. "But thanks for missing that goal!"

Kat bit her lip. She grabbed a handful of grass and tossed it up at Luke. As he swatted it away, Kat swung her arm playfully behind his legs and knocked into the back of his knees. He flailed back and forth for a moment and then dropped to the ground.

Kat smiled. "Oh, sorry!" she said. "I was just stretching. How many goals did *you* score?"

Luke held his hands up. "None," he admitted. "But maybe you *should* work on your shooting."

Kat flopped on her back and looked up at the sky. "I have been!" she said.

"You've seen me practicing after dinner. What more can I do?"

"I don't know, but you need to find a way to get better before Alex Akers comes for the big game," Luke said.

Luke and Kat's mom was friends with Alex Akers, the women's soccer star. They had played soccer together in college. Alex was coming to stay with Luke and Kat's family in two weeks to watch Kat's big game. Alex was on the Breakers, the best team in women's soccer. She had won the Player of the Year award for the last three years.

Alice tapped Kat on the knee. "Why don't you ask Alex to help you work on your shooting?" she asked. "Maybe she'd give you some tips."

Kat sat up. "That's a great idea!" she said. A big smile spread across her face. She jumped up and did a couple of air kicks. "Zap! Zam! Another goal by Alex Akers!" She kicked again. "And one by Kat!"

"Hey, maybe I can get some pointers, too!" Luke said.

"No!" Kat said. "You don't always have to do everything that *I* do. Your team isn't playing in the big game. If you go near her, I'll give *you* a shot!"

"Oh yeah?" Luke asked. He hitched his shoulders back and turned to face Kat. "Just try to stop me. . . ."

Alice laughed and jumped in between them. "Hey, maybe she'll have time to give you *both* some soccer tips," she said. Alice tugged Kat's arm. "We need to get over to the field house for our ride."

Alice, Luke, and Kat gathered their things and ran to catch up with their friends. Max and Nico were standing in front of the field house, at the corner of the soccer field. The field house was an old two-story building. It had been used for summer camps and storing athletic equipment, but the town closed it a few years ago because it needed repairs.

"Alice, when's your dad getting here?" Max said. He was kicking a soccer ball against the side of the field house.

"About ten minutes," Alice said.

Just then, a kid from the boys' soccer team walked by with his father, who was also the boys' soccer coach. They were headed to their car.

"Hey, Danny," Nico said. "Nice goal in today's game!"

Danny gave a thumbs-up. "Thanks," he said. "But I'm still not as good as you, Nico!" Nico was one of the best athletes in the school.

"Hey, Alice and Kat, good game!" Danny's father, Mr. Danforth, said. He was a tall man with short black hair. Even when he was coaching, he always wore a suit and tie.

Danny got into the car with his father, and they drove away.

"Isn't Mr. Danforth trying to tear down the field house?" Alice asked.

Kat nodded. "The town doesn't have enough money to fix it, and Mr. Danforth wants to build an office building," Kat said. "My mom's in a group trying to save it."

Nico looked up at the front of the building. It needed a good painting, and half the shutters were missing. "It's too bad," he said.

While they waited for Alice's father, Max and Nico took turns trying to hit a spot on the wall with the soccer ball. Nico was definitely a better shot, but Max was having fun kicking the ball as hard as he could.

A few minutes later, the kids heard a door slam shut across the street. An older man with a hat had just left his house to walk his dog.

"It's Mr. Jennings," Alice said. "Maybe he'll come over here with Sammy."

"Mr. Jennings is the one who's always mean to kids," Max said.

"I know," Alice said. "But his dog,

Sammy, is nice. I'm going to see if I can pet him."

Alice loved all types of animals. Even though she had three dogs at home, she was always excited to see other dogs or cats. When Mr. Jennings reached the sidewalk in front of the field house, Alice ran over to pet Sammy. She returned a few minutes later when Mr. Jennings continued on his walk.

"Hey, Alice, watch this!" Max called out as she came back. He trapped the soccer ball and pulled his leg back to kick as hard as he could.

WHAP!

Max whacked the ball with his foot. But instead of kicking it straight on, he caught the edge of the ball and it sliced to the right.

"Oh no!" Max called out. "Stop it!"

But it was too late.

CRASH!

The ball smashed through the front window of the field house!

ALICE'S BIG IDEA

"I can't believe you did that!" Alice said to Max.

The soccer ball had broken a first-floor window and sailed into the field house.

"I'd say that kick was a *smashing* success, Max," Luke said with a grin. "I think you *shattered* our team record for the hardest kick!"

Nico ran over to the window and looked in on his tiptoes. "I don't see the ball," he said. Then he reached through the broken window. He easily moved the inside latch and carefully slid the lower part of the window up. "I'm going to find the soccer ball," he said.

Max ran over to Nico.

"Wait, isn't that breaking and entering?" Kat asked. "Maybe we should tell the police."

"Well, we're not going to hurt anything," Max said. "We're just going to get the soccer ball back."

While Kat and Max were talking, Nico had slipped through the window. He reached his hand out. "Here, come help me find the ball," he said. Nico helped pull them through the window one after another.

It took a moment for their eyes to adjust to the darkness of the field house. But as they did, the kids could make out the features of the room.

"Wow!" Max said. "It looks like no one's been in here for a long time."

A layer of dust covered the floor and the bookcases against the wall.

"This is like that haunted house we made in my basement," Nico said. "Remember the maze we had and how we popped out and scared people?"

Just then, Luke gasped. "Look out for the rat!" he yelled.

Suddenly, something flew across the room at Max.

"Gross!" Max cried. He swatted it out of the air and jumped back as it fell to the floor.

"What is it?" Alice called.

Max slowly leaned over to examine what was at his feet. Then he picked it up and burst out laughing. He threw it at Luke.

"Nice try, Luke," Max said. "But the only 'rat' around here is you!"

"Ha-ha! I knew I'd get you," Luke said. He picked up the "rat" and showed it to the others. It was an old sock that

he had found in the corner. "Anyone else afraid of the rat?" he asked.

Everyone laughed.

"I remember going to summer camp here," Kat said. "We used to do arts and crafts on the table in the corner."

"I can't believe that Mr. Danforth wants to tear this down," Alice said. "Why can't they just fix it up?"

Kat shook her head. "They tried to do that, but it's too expensive," she said. "My mother said she doesn't think there's any way to save the building. Mr. Danforth said he'd replace it with a nice office building and it would look a lot better."

"Hey, come here," Nico called. He had passed through the back room of the field house to another room. It looked like an old kitchen.

"This would make a really cool snack bar," he said when the others arrived. "Wouldn't it be great if there was a window where you could walk up and buy food when you were playing soccer or football? And maybe instead of just cookies and candy, they could sell some of my secret trail mix or special vegetable zingers!"

In addition to being one of the school's best athletes, Nico was also one of its best eaters. He liked to experiment at home and come up with new healthy snacks. He always had a new recipe for something that would make him stronger or faster.

"Yeah," Max said. "We could call it Nico's Superfoods for Super Athletes! But do you have any foods that will give us superpowers to find the soccer ball?"

Nico laughed. "Okay, you're right. Let's keep going," he said.

The group passed through a long room that ran along the side of the building.

"Look at this," Alice said. "If Nico can have a snack bar, then I'm going to turn this room into a golfing area. We can set up a couple of those big nets and special video screens that you can hit golf balls into to practice. We used them on vacation last year, and they were so much fun!"

"That would be great!" Nico said. "Maybe if you did that, I could make cheesy popcorn snacks that would look like golf balls!"

"We don't need golf balls," Max said as they made it back to the front room. "We need to find my soccer ball."

"It couldn't have gone far," Nico said. "It's got to be here somewhere."

They split up and searched all around the room. Kat finally spotted the ball wedged behind a couch.

"Got it!" she called. Kat picked up the soccer ball and handed it back to Max. Then they quickly climbed out the window to wait for Alice's father. On the way, Nico found an old piece of wood. He brought it out with him. After everyone was outside, Nico wedged the board in front of the window.

Alice checked the time. "Dad should be here soon," she said.

Kat studied the field house and let out a sigh. "I really wish there was some way to save this place and fix it up. It could be so cool!" she said.

Max returned to kicking his soccer ball against the side of the building.

Alice watched Max for a moment. Then a thought hit her.

"Max, that's it!" Alice said. "What if we use soccer to stop Mr. Danforth from tearing down the field house?"

AN ANGRY CUSTOMER

"What do you mean?" Luke asked.

"Maybe we can get Alex Akers to help us save the field house," Alice said.

"But she plays soccer," Luke said. "She's not a construction worker!"

Alice shook her head. "We don't need Alex to help fix it up," she said. "We need her to help raise money! Alex is famous. We could organize a fund-raiser on the day of the game, and Alex could be the star attraction. It would be a great project for the MVP Club!"

The kids had just formed a club

called the MVP Club. They had been awarded Most Valuable Player medals by the principal for figuring out who had messed up the Franklin School Olympics.

"Wow, great idea, Alice," Max said. "Maybe Alex can play goalie and people can try to score a goal against her. Who wouldn't like a chance to sneak one by Alex Akers?"

"That's a great idea!" Kat said. "She usually plays striker, so it would be fun to see her in the goal for a change."

A car horn beeped. Alice's father had just pulled up in his green minivan.

"I'll talk to my mom tonight," Kat said. "Keep your fingers crossed!"

The next day after school, Kat and Luke bounded outside to catch up with Alice, Max, and Nico.

"GOOOOAAAALLLL!" Luke said.

"Kat called Alex Akers last night. She said she'd be happy to help us!"

The kids slapped high fives all around.

"That'll be really cool," Max said. "I'll bet I can distract her and get a nice easy one in the net."

"Oh yeah?" Luke said. "Nice and easy like knocking that window out yesterday?"

"Hey!" Kat said. "Stop fooling around. We have two weeks to try to save the field house."

The MVP Club spent the next ten days working on the fund-raiser. They started by getting approval from the town to hold the event. Then they handed out flyers to let people know about it. The club had even organized a bake sale at school and convinced other Franklin students to post signs all around town.

On Thursday, two days before the fund-raiser and the game, Nico, Alice, and Luke headed straight to the big

supermarket after school. Luke and Kat's mother helped them set up a table right outside the entrance. Then she went inside to shop.

They put the cardboard model of the field house that Kat had made on the table. Kat loved doing art projects, so she had all the special cardboard, glue, and paint that she needed to create a model that looked real.

For the next two hours, they handed out flyers and collected donations. When it was almost time to go, Nico picked up the donation box. "Today was good, but I think it's all going to come down to how much money we raise on Saturday. If we don't make enough, there's no way the town can fix up the field house."

They were just getting ready to go home when another shopper came out.

"It's Mr. Jennings!" Alice whispered to Nico. "He's the guy with the dog who lives across from the field house."

Mr. Jennings stopped at the table and rested his shopping bag on the ground. He looked down his nose at the model and then pulled a pack of gum out of his pocket. It was the new Kiwi-Berri brand with the bright pink and green stripes. Mr. Jennings slid out a stick of gum and unwrapped it. He balled up the colorful wrapper and tossed it on the table. Then he pointed to the model.

"What's that?" he asked.

Nico explained about the fund-raiser to save the field house.

Mr. Jennings snorted. "Sorry, kids, but I wouldn't give you a dime to save that field house," he said. "I can't wait for the city to finally sell it. It's ugly and old."

Nico, Alice, and Luke looked at each other.

Mr. Jennings picked up his shopping bag and turned to go. "I hope they tear it down," he muttered. "I can't wait to see that old building gone!"

A RED-HOT PRACTICE

"Well, maybe not everyone wants to save the field house," Nico said.

"Mr. Jennings must have picked up some grumpy pills in addition to his groceries," Luke said.

"At least his dog is nice," Alice said. "But I can't believe that people still litter."

Luke picked up the bright pink-and-green gum wrapper that Mr. Jennings had left behind. He tried to wrap it around his finger like a ring and showed it to Alice. The pink and green stripes stood out.

"Very nice, Luke, but I don't think we can get any money for a ring," Alice said. "Anyway, we got a lot of other donations today. Alex Akers is going to be impressed. I can't wait for our practice with her tomorrow."

The next day, the kids flew out of school when the last bell rang. They ran to the bike racks, hopped on their bikes, and rode over to the soccer field.

They spotted Alex at the far end of the field. She was dribbling a ball back and forth and taking shots on goal. The kids raced over and watched quietly until she finished practicing.

"Oh, hi, guys," Alex called out. She picked up her soccer ball and jogged over to them. Alex had short blond hair and was wearing a soccer jersey and white shorts. She had on bright purple-and-green soccer cleats.

"Wow! Cool cleats," Kat said.

Alex smiled. "Yup, that's one of the perks of playing professional soccer," she said. "We get to try out all kinds of new shoes."

Kat introduced Alex to the rest of the MVP Club.

"Awesome! So, is everyone ready?" Alex asked. "I know that Alice and Kat have an important game tomorrow, so we're going to do a lot of work today. Now it's time to get down to some professional soccer!" She blew a whistle and lined the kids up on the side of the field.

Alex had them spend the next hour doing dribbling, shooting, and passing drills. Then she let them take a "break" by having them play goalie and try to stop her from scoring. Each kid took a turn, but Alex went past them and easily took shots on an empty net.

Kat waited until last to go. Alex lined up at the halfway line. Kat stood in front of the goalposts. She danced back and forth on her feet, ready to defend the goal. She clenched and unclenched her hands.

Alex dribbled the ball forward, slowly at first. Then she sped up and zipped to the right. Kat moved to follow the ball.

Alex skittered the other way and pounded a shot with her foot.

Kat tried to move back into a good position, but was she too late? The ball was heading straight for the outside corner of the net.

Kat jumped and dove as hard as she could. She stretched her fingers out. It was going to be close.

The ball grazed her fingertips as it sailed right past the post!

Kat had stopped Alex's goal! She fell to the ground, out of breath.

A cheer went up from the rest of the MVP Club. They had been watching from the sidelines.

"Way to go, Kat!" Nico said. "Awesome save!"

"You're the only one who was able to stop Alex," Max called. "You're the soccer star now!"

"That *was* a really good save, Kat," Alex called as she picked up the ball.

After a short break, Alex ran them through more drills. She spent some of the time working with Kat while Nico, Luke, Max, and Alice had a short scrimmage.

"If you see the goalie run at you when you're about to shoot, use a chip shot," Alex said to Kat. "Angle the top part of your toe down to hit the ball at the bottom. It'll 'chip' the ball over the

goalie and into the net." Alex showed her how to do it a few times and then had Kat practice the shot.

After a little while longer, everyone took a break. The kids were hot and sweaty. But Kat had a huge smile on her face.

Everyone sat on the grass at the side of the field, under the shade of a big maple tree. Alex dragged a heavy cooler over to them and opened its top. "I figured you'd be thirsty," she said. "So I brought along some PowerPunch!"

"Awesome!" Nico said. "I'll take a red one."

The cooler was filled with ice and tall bottles of red, green, and orange PowerPunch sports drink. The kids dug through the cooler until they found their favorite flavors. They pulled the bottles out and took long swigs.

"Hey, look," Max said after he was done with his first sip. "There's a picture of Alex on the bottle!" Underneath the picture on each bottle, it read *Soccer star Alex Akers gets a real kick out of PowerPunch!*

Alex laughed. "Yes, that's another perk of being a soccer player. We get to do some exciting things."

As everyone spread out on the grass to rest, Nico moved back toward the center of the field. He stared at the field house for a few minutes.

"Hey, is that smoke coming from the side of the field house?" Nico called out.

Alex and the kids jumped up and

ran over. Nico pointed to the right side of the field house. But nobody else saw smoke or anything strange.

"Maybe it was just leaves or dust, Nico," Alex said. "Let's finish up practice. You girls are in great shape for your game tomorrow. But maybe you can all help me practice for the fund-raiser, since I usually don't play goalie. You kick the balls, and I'll try to stop them!"

They went one after the other. On Kat's turn, Alex gave her some tips. She didn't score a goal, but she got really close.

After Kat came Alice. Alex stopped her shot, too. As Alice jogged back to get in line again, Nico was getting ready at midfield. But just as he was about to start dribbling the soccer ball, Alice stopped him. Her eyes were wide. She started hopping up and down and pointed.

"Look! Nico was right!" Alice called. "The field house is burning down!"

A SURPRISING SUSPECT

Everyone turned to look. Alice was right! Bright yellow and orange flames were shooting out of the right side of the field house!

Alice nudged Max. "Quick. Call 9-1-1," she said.

Max ran to the side of the field and fumbled through the pockets of his sweatshirt. He pulled out his phone to report the fire.

When he finished the call, the group ran down to the far end of the field. As they drew closer, they could see the flames coming out of a wooden shed next to the field house.

A few seconds later, they heard sirens wailing. A police car screeched to a halt at the corner. Two police officers jumped out. A policewoman stepped into the street to direct traffic while a policeman walked up to the growing crowd.

"Please take a few steps back," he called as he waved his arms. "We want to keep everyone safe and give the firefighters room to work."

Alex and the kids moved back about twenty feet. The flames shot higher.

More sirens wailed. Two big red fire trucks stopped in front of the field house. Firefighters with thick coats and metal hats jumped out. A tall firefighter grabbed a hose and ran to a fire hydrant down the street. Others pulled hoses around the side of the building and

started shooting jets of water at the flames.

It didn't take the firefighters long to get the fire under control. Even after the fire was out a few minutes later, the firefighters continued to shoot water on the smoldering side of the building.

"I'm going to call your mom, Kat," Alex said. "Just so she knows we're all safe."

As Alex took a short walk away from all the action, the kids inched closer to

the fire for a better look. The smell of burned wood lingered in the air. The firefighters had started to lay out their hoses and roll them up.

"Okay, folks, time to head home," the policeman said. "The fire's out and the action's over."

The kids turned to go, but Max stopped them. "Don't you guys ever read mystery books?" he said. "This fire is suspicious. Why would the field house suddenly catch fire just before the fund-raiser? I'll bet someone did it on purpose!"

"Max, just because you want to be a detective when you grow up doesn't mean that everything's a mystery!" Alice said.

Max shook his head. "I think something's up," he said. "We can't leave now. We need to investigate."

"But how?" Kat asked. "They just told us to go home."

"Since my dad's a detective, he knows all the firefighters and police officers," Max said. "I'm going to talk to them."

Kat and the others followed as Max walked over to a firefighter with a big gold shield on the front of his helmet. The gold shield read *Fire Chief.* The man was watching the other firefighters put away the equipment.

"Excuse me," Max said as he got near.

"I'm Max. My dad's Detective Samson.
We were playing soccer when we saw
the flames, so we called 9-1-1."

"Oh, so you're the Max I always hear
about," the fire chief said. "I'm Chief
George. Your father tells me you'll make
a good detective when you grow up."

"Do you know how it started?" Max asked.

"We don't know exactly what caused it," the chief said. "But the fire started in a small shed on the side of the building. It's the only thing that burned. Now, if you'll excuse me, I have to get back to work. It was nice meeting you, Max."

The kids said goodbye and went back to find Alex. She had finished her phone call with Kat and Luke's mom.

"We're going to get our bikes and ride home," Kat said.

"Okay," Alex said. She gave Kat a fist bump. "That was exciting. But not as exciting as your soccer game is going to be tomorrow! You did a great job today, Kat!"

Kat smiled. "Thanks!" she said. "We'll see you back at our house."

The kids walked to their bikes as Alex left in her car.

"We should investigate the fire," Max

said. "Let's meet here tomorrow morning before the fund-raiser."

"Okay," Nico said. "But it seems like a stretch that someone would burn down the field house on purpose."

Max shook his head. "Not if someone is afraid we'll save it!" he said.

"But that doesn't make sense," Nico said. "If we save it, the town will fix it up and everyone wins."

A big grin crossed Max's face. "Unless someone wants to build something else there," he said. "Like an office building!"

Alice pulled her shoulders back. "You're crazy!" she said. "You think that Mr. Danforth tried to burn the field house down? Why would he do that?"

"It all makes sense. If the field house is gone, the town will have to sell him the land," Max said. "Then he can build his big new office building!"

A BAD NEIGHBOR

The next morning, a faint whiff of burned wood still floated over the soccer field. Yellow police tape had been strung around the burned-out shed.

"Okay, we don't have much time," Alice said as they locked up their bikes. "Let's take a look around and then start getting ready for the fund-raiser."

The kids couldn't get too close because of the police tape. They could see the charred remains of the small shed where the fire had started. But the main part of the building wasn't damaged.

The MVP Club spread out and started checking the ground near the police tape. They looked for anything that the police might have missed. But all they saw was soggy grass and burned embers until Luke spotted something.

"Look! I've found a clue!" he called out. The others came running over.

Luke picked something up from the ground. He held it out in the palm of his hand for the others to see.

It was a small pink-and-green piece of paper.

"That looks like the gum wrapper that Mr. Jennings dropped on our table!" Alice said.

"It is." Luke nodded. "I remember it from when I picked it up yesterday."

"And look," Nico said. "It's wet. That means it was probably here before the firefighters shot all the water on the fire. That means it wasn't dropped here this morning."

"Then maybe it was Mr. Jennings and not Mr. Danforth who set the fire!" Max said. "Mr. Jennings hates the field house! He even told us he couldn't wait to see the building gone."

"Yeah," Nico said. "He was worried we'd save it, so he tried to burn it down. But we stopped him!"

Alice glanced at the other side of the field. Kat's mom had just pulled up. She and Alex were starting to walk from the car to the field.

"Hey, we have to go help set up," Alice said. "What do we do about Mr. Jennings?"

"We can tell a police officer when they get here," Max said. "I bet some of them will come to the fund-raiser with their families."

The MVP Club ran across the field to help unload stuff from the car. They pulled out a bag of soccer balls they had borrowed from the school. Nico and Max grabbed a long table and a few chairs. They set them up on the sideline. They put out Kat's model of the field house. Kat had even cut a slot in the roof so that people could drop their money right in!

While they waited for people to show up, Alex had the kids practice. After running up and down the field twice to warm up, Alex took her place in front of the goal. The MVP Club all lined up and tried to sneak shots past her. But Alex blocked them all.

Soon, other kids and parents arrived. Many brought cookies, popcorn, and oranges for the bake sale.

Alex got ready for the fund-raiser while the kids helped out at the tables they had set up. Nico and Max sat at the bake sale table. Alice took a seat behind

the donation table. She wrote down people's names as they dropped money into the model of the field house. Then Kat or Luke would lead each person to the center of the soccer field for a chance to take a shot on goal.

Kat and Luke had fun as they watched Alex stop lots of shots. Every now and then, someone would get lucky and sneak one in. When they

did, Alex would run forward, shake the person's hand, and give them a signed picture from a bag near the goal. Everyone seemed happy to try their luck against one of the best soccer players of all time.

The fund-raiser was going great. Lots of people were lined up to take shots at Alex. Every time Alex stopped a ball, the crowd cheered. Once people took their turn, they would buy food from the bake sale table or just hang out and talk. Everyone was talking about the fire at the field house.

The fund-raiser had been going on almost an hour when Max finally spotted a policewoman near the edge of the field. He asked Kat's mom to take over at the bake sale, and motioned for his friends to come with him.

"Excuse me," Max said when they reached the policewoman. "We think we know who started the field house fire!"

The policewoman looked down at them. "You do?" she asked. "What do you know about it?"

Max told the policewoman what had happened at the supermarket with Mr. Jennings. Then he explained how they had seen the fire and investigated it this morning, and how Luke had found a matching gum wrapper near the burned-out shed.

"We think Mr. Jennings did it!" Max concluded.

The policewoman nodded. "I'll have to say, you kids are pretty smart," she said.

Luke looked at Alice and Max. "What do you mean?" he said.

The policewoman smiled. "You're right about the clue," she said. "Mr. Jennings did start the fire!"

SOMETHING FISHY AT THE FIELD HOUSE

"I can't believe it," Max said. "We were right!"

The members of the MVP Club gave each other high fives. "Are you going to arrest Mr. Jennings?" Kat asked.

The police officer shook her head. "No," she said. "We're not."

The high fives stopped. They all stared at her.

"What?" Kat asked. "He almost burned the field house down!"

The policewoman shook her head.

"We know he started the fire," she said,
"but he didn't do it on purpose."

"But he hates the field house!" Max
said. "He told us he wanted it gone."

"I know he doesn't like the field
house. He complained about it at town
council meetings last year. But the fire
was an accident," the policewoman said.

"Mr. Jennings was out walking yesterday when he thought he heard somebody in the shed. He's been keeping an eye on the place ever since someone broke the front window a few weeks ago."

The kids all looked at Max. He shrugged. But the policewoman didn't notice.

"How did the fire start?" Nico asked.

"Mr. Jennings went into the shed to check on the noise. It was dark, and he tripped on some wires. They sparked, and it started a small fire. He tried to put the fire out with his feet but couldn't. That's when he rushed home to call us."

"But *we* saw the fire first," Max said. "And *I* called 9-1-1!"

"You kids did an amazing job of notifying us right away," the policewoman said. "But Mr. Jennings called at the same time. He told the 9-1-1 operator he had started the fire and how it happened."

Max kicked at the grass with his

sneaker. "I don't believe it," he said. "Mr. Jennings must have thought that we saw him start the fire or something, so he pretended it was an accident."

The policewoman smiled. "Come on," she said. "You kids did some really good detective work. And you were right! But Mr. Jennings isn't a criminal, even if he wants the field house gone. Thanks for trying to help."

"Argh! We were so close!" Max said as the policewoman walked away. "I knew that clue was real!"

"At least you were *almost* right, Max," Alice said.

Nico clapped his hands. "The only way we're going to stop Mr. Danforth is to get back to the fund-raiser and make more money," he said. "Who's ready to donate and try to score against Alex?"

Everybody raised a hand.

"Come on," Nico said. He ran over to the donation table. Everyone followed his lead as he pulled out some money. Once they stuffed their bills into Kat's field house model, they lined up on the sideline.

After they waited for the people in front of them to go, it was Nico's turn. As soon as the whistle blew, he zoomed up the field, dodging left and right. Alex watched him like a hawk. When he finally kicked the ball, it sailed straight for the top left corner of the goal. But

Alex was there and tipped it away.

Nico still looked determined as he jogged off the field. He slapped Max's hand as he passed by. "I'm going to get more money to try again," Nico said. "I know I can do it next time."

One after another, Max, Luke, and Alice went up against Alex. Each time, she stopped their soccer balls before they were even close to scoring. Finally, it was

Kat's turn. She took the ball at midfield and ran toward the goal with it. She headed straight for Alex. But at the last moment, she zipped to the right and nailed the ball, just like Alex had taught her. Instead of flying straight, it bent around Alex, even though she jumped to stop it. The ball was headed for the side of the goal!

Max, Alice, and Luke held their breath. Would Kat be the first one of them to score against Alex?

No. The ball sailed right into the goalpost and bounced back into Alex's hands. Kat hadn't scored.

Kat shuffled back to the group.

"Don't worry," Alice said. "You'll do better in the game. That was an awesome kick. You got it around Alex perfectly!"

"I know," Kat said. "But I didn't make the goal, just like the last game."

The kids watched as the last few people took their turns against Alex. The fund-raiser was almost over. The girls' soccer game was scheduled to start in fifteen minutes.

They wandered back to the donation table. Kat's mom held up Kat's field house model. "This is almost full! You kids did a great job!"

"I'll say," said Mr. Danforth, who was standing nearby. "I'm not sure you've raised enough to save the field house, but here's a bit more."

Kat looked at the others. None of them knew what to say. They watched

as he stuffed the money into the model of the field house.

"Good luck," Mr. Danforth said, and then walked away. He started to head toward the field house but then stopped to make a phone call.

"What was that?" Alice asked. "Why would Mr. Danforth donate money to us?"

Before anyone could answer, they heard Alex's whistle. The fund-raiser was over! Alex ran off the field to cheers. She slapped outstretched hands as she jogged back to the donation table. When she got there, the kids all cheered.

Alice and Kat's teammate Tasha came over and tapped them on the shoulders. "Coach wants us to warm up," she said. "Get your cleats and shin guards on and meet us under the tree over there."

"Okay," Alice said. She and Kat picked up their equipment and headed for the tree. Max, Luke, and Nico waited near the sidelines as the girls practiced.

They watched the Warriors go through their drills on the backup field.

All the while, Max kept glancing across the field at something. Finally, just as the referee blew her whistle, Max nudged Nico and Luke.

"Come on," he said. "Something's up. We have to go."

Nico looked at Max. "What do you mean? Now?"

"We've got to get to the field house," Max said. "Mr. Danforth is heading over there."

"But what about the game?" Luke asked. "Kat and Alice are almost ready to play!"

Max tugged on their shirts. "We'll be back soon," he said. "But we need to follow Mr. Danforth to make sure he doesn't try to do something like burn it down!"

A NEAR MISS

As the girls ran to the soccer field, the boys headed for the field house.

They crept through the fans crowding the sidelines. Ahead of them, Mr. Danforth was cutting briskly across the grass.

When they got halfway to the field house, Max stopped near a tree along the road. He called Nico and Luke over. They huddled behind the tree, out of sight.

Mr. Danforth approached the front of the field house. They watched as he walked over to the window that Max had knocked out with the soccer ball. He waited until two cars passed by. As soon as the coast was clear, Mr. Danforth reached up and pulled down the board that Nico had put over the broken window!

Nico and Luke gasped as they watched Mr. Danforth climb through the window.

"What's he doing?" Nico asked.

"Maybe he's planning on finishing the job Mr. Jennings started," Nico said. "Either way, we've got to keep an eye on him! Let's go!"

The boys ran over to the field house. They walked up to the broken window and peeked inside. The room was empty. There was no sign of Mr. Danforth.

"Come on!" Nico whispered. He put his gymnastics skills to good use and hopped through the window like a

rabbit. Then he reached out and pulled Luke and Max in.

Once inside, they stayed near the wall and tiptoed over to the doorway to the back room. They listened for a minute, trying to hear Mr. Danforth, but they couldn't. Finally, Nico peeked through the doorframe into the kitchen area. That room was empty, too.

"Maybe he went upstairs," Nico whispered.

They kept going through the rooms. They paused before checking each one, but Mr. Danforth wasn't in any of them. The only place left to check was upstairs.

They quietly made their way to the stairs. Nico was just about to climb the first step when Max accidentally bumped the banister. A big, round wooden ball at the end of it popped off.

THUNK! The wooden ball landed on the floor with a crash.

Nico and Luke both looked at Max.

"What's that?" said a voice from the top of the stairs. The kids looked up.

It was Mr. Danforth!

"What are you kids doing here?" he asked. "I thought you were at the fundraiser."

"Um, um . . ." Max nodded. "We were, but then we saw you come down here. When you came in, we had to check and make sure everything was all right!"

"Yeah," Luke said. "Mr. Jennings almost burned this place down yesterday. We wanted to make sure *no other accidents happened.*"

Mr. Danforth stared at them for a moment. And then he laughed. He started down the stairs.

"You don't think I'm going to burn the place down, do you?" he asked.

Max, Nico, and Luke looked at each other.

Max cleared his throat. "Um, we didn't know what you were doing here," he said. "That's why we wanted to check."

Mr. Danforth nodded as he reached the last step. "I get it," he said. "It's good to keep an eye on things. I just wanted to come over here before the game to think for a minute. I've spent a lot of time working on new plans for this place. I can't wait for the meeting with the town council this week."

Max's eyes narrowed. "We know all about that meeting," he said. "Kat and Luke are going to be there with their mom. They're going to present the money we've collected. If only the town knew all the cool things they could do with this old field house."

"What do you mean?" Mr. Danforth asked. "Like what?"

Max stood up a little straighter. "Well, um, a few of us were in here a while ago looking around," he said. "And we noticed that the field house could be turned into a real community center. Kids could come, and there would be good food and sports equipment for playing. It just needs some fixing up."

"We can show you," Nico said. "Come to the kitchen."

When they got there, Nico pointed out how they could make a cool snack bar for the recreation fields. Maybe visitors could try Nico's special vegetable zingers. Next, Max led them into the side porch area. He told Mr. Danforth that they thought about making a golf practice room out of it.

Mr. Danforth walked to one side of the room. He settled his feet in position and took a few big swings with a pretend golf club. Then he studied the room and nodded. "I could see that," he said. "If we set this up as a golf practice range, a lot of people might use it."

They continued through all the rooms on the first floor. As they walked from room to room, Max kept talking and Mr. Danforth kept nodding.

All of a sudden, they heard a loud cheer outside.

"Hey, we have to get back to the soccer game," Luke said.

Nico nodded. He checked the time. "Wow, you're right!" he said. "They're probably almost finished with the first half." Nico headed for the front window.

"Sorry, but we should go," Max said as Nico and Luke crawled out the window.

"That's fine," Mr. Danforth said. He waved to them. "You don't have to worry about me here. I'm just going to think a little more. Thanks for the tour. It was very interesting."

Once they were outside, Max, Nico, and Luke ran back to the soccer field. Nico had been right. There was only five minutes left in first half of the game. But Alice and Kat's team was losing 0–1.

The Franklin girls had just taken possession of the ball. The Franklin School students and parents were going wild cheering.

Max, Nico, and Luke pushed their

way through the crowd until they found a spot up near the halfway line.

The girls moved the ball up the field. They looked in control. They made pass after pass, and the other team seemed tired from running after the ball. But then a redheaded girl from the Warriors intercepted a pass and dribbled back downfield with it. She streaked down the left side, passing Franklin midfielders and defenders. As she neared the corner flag, she drove a long crossing pass toward her teammates in front of Franklin's goal. A Warriors player jumped high in the air. She smacked her head into the incoming ball and sent it toward the upper corner of the goal. But at the last second, Franklin's goalie hurled herself up and snagged the ball.

Franklin's goalie waited for the players to spread out, and then she threw the ball downfield. It landed right in front of Tasha, who dribbled it for a few feet and passed it to Alice.

Again, the Franklin girls moved the ball toward the other team's goal. They passed it back and forth easily as the crowd cheered.

With seconds left, Tasha passed the ball to Kat. There would only be time for one chance at a goal before the whistle blew.

Kat raced toward the goal with the ball. One of the Warriors headed right for her, but Kat spun around and moved past her. She cut past another defender who tried to win the ball back. Now there was nothing between her and the goal except the goalie.

Kat wound up and kicked the ball. It sailed right toward the top corner of the goal!

The crowd held its breath. They

waited to see if the ball would slide into the net.

But it didn't.

The soccer ball hit the top post of the goal and bounced up and over it. The referee's whistle blew. The half was over. Franklin was still behind. Kat had blown Franklin's chance to tie the game.

THE FINAL KICK

The Franklin girls slumped off the field. Ms. Suraci, the team's coach, gathered them in a huddle for a quick pep talk and then let them take a break for oranges and water.

"Oh, that's too bad," Luke said. "Kat had been working so hard on her shooting."

"But she was really close," Max said. "Let's go over and try to cheer her up."

Max, Nico, and Luke wound through the crowd of fans. Many of them had headed to the bake sale table or were hanging out in the shade of the nearby maple trees. The three boys found Kat and Alice resting on the grass.

"Kat, that was a nice try," Max said. "You almost had it!"

Kat hung her head. "It's just the same problem all over again," she said. "I should have tied the game."

"You *will* tie the game," said a voice from behind them. It was Alex. She walked over to Kat and hunched down. She patted Kat's back.

"You have great form!" Alex said. "All you need to do is make sure your knee is over the ball when you shoot. That way you'll be right on target. And don't forget that chip shot I taught you if the goalie comes out of the net. It's harder in the middle of a game than in practice, but don't let that stop you. You can do it!"

Kat smiled. "Okay," she said.

"Just go out there for the second half and pretend it's a practice with me," Alex said. "You'll do great."

Alex gave Kat a high five and stood up. A few minutes later, the coach called the girls to huddle again. They talked for a while and then took the field for the second half with big whoops.

When the whistle blew, the Franklin girls got off to a good start. They moved the ball downfield toward the Warriors' goal. Alice took a shot, but the Warriors goalie stopped it.

A few plays later, a Franklin defender fouled a Warriors attacker who was dribbling in the penalty area. The ref held out her hand and pointed to the ground. She

was giving the Warriors a penalty kick!

The Warriors player who had been fouled got set and kicked the ball to the left. The Franklin goalie dove to the right but missed it.

Another goal for the Warriors! Now they were ahead 0–2!

Each team ran to its side of the field for the kickoff. The referee placed the ball on the center spot in the middle of the field. Tasha from Franklin's team stepped up to the ball. When the referee blew her whistle, Tasha pushed the ball to Alice.

"Shift with the ball, Alice! Go, Franklin!" Alex shouted from the sidelines.

Alice and her teammates brought the ball up the field. When they got close to the Warriors' goal, Shauna had the ball. She ran toward the goalie and a line of Warriors defenders. Right as she was about to run into them, she brought her leg back like she was going to shoot, but instead of kicking the ball, she tapped it to Tasha. Shauna had tricked the Warriors! Nobody was in front of Tasha to stop her. She dribbled it once and then smashed the ball directly into the net!

Franklin had scored! But they were still down by one.

With five minutes left in the game, the teams were tired. Unless Franklin could find some extra energy, it looked like the Warriors might win.

On their next possession, Franklin seemed to find a spark. Tasha threw the ball in, and Alice ran hard up the field.

"Out wide! Out wide!" Alex called.

Alice dribbled the ball expertly and easily went around two tall Warriors. Although she wasn't very close to the goal, Alice saw an opening and belted the ball. It was a hard-driving shot. It lifted slightly off the ground and sailed through the air. By the time the Warriors goalie spotted it, it was too late.

The ball flew past her and into the net!

Another goal for Franklin! The game was tied! The Franklin team exploded in cheers.

But time was starting to run out. Franklin would need to score again in order to win the game or it would go into overtime.

The Warriors passed the ball back and forth, up the field. They charged toward Franklin's goal. A tall girl with glasses wove through Franklin's defense and took a powerful shot at the goal. But Franklin's goalie blocked it.

"I'll bet the regular time will end in a tie," Max said to Nico and Luke. They nodded in agreement.

The game was coming down to its final minutes.

Tasha passed the ball to Kat. She ran it up the field straight for the goal. But one of the Warriors slid in and knocked the ball out of bounds!

TWEEEET!

The referee stopped the game.

"Woo-hoo! You can do it, Franklin!" Alex shouted from the sideline.

Kat went to the edge of the field and threw the ball in. She was aiming for Alice, but one of the Warriors players intercepted it!

"Oh no!" Luke cried. "That's gonna be it for Franklin! I don't think they'll have another chance!"

The Warriors passed the ball back and forth to move downfield. One of their players was just setting up for a shot on goal when Kat emerged from behind her. Kat knocked the ball away with her right foot and zoomed up the field with it. Most of the Warriors were still down at the other end of the field when Kat came in close to their goal.

She was going to have the last play of the game. There were only seconds left. It was all up to Kat.

She raced for the goal. Suddenly, the Warriors goalie came sprinting toward her. Kat had to make up her mind fast or else the goalie would get the ball! Just as the goalie dove at her feet, Kat kicked at the bottom of the ball, with her foot pointed toward the ground.

Max, Nico, Luke, and the rest of the crowd went nuts screaming and yelling.

Kat's ball arced high in the air, over the goalie and toward the top of the crossbar.

The kids held their breath.

Kat clenched her hands.

The ball sailed past the top bar of the goalpost.

But this time it was underneath!

The ball bounced into the back of the Warriors' net.

Kat had scored!

The ref's whistle blew. The game was over.

Franklin had won!

The crowd erupted in cheers. Nico, Max, and Luke jumped up and down and screamed.

"She did it!" Luke yelled. "My sister won the game! Go, Kat!"

As fans flooded the field, Kat ran over to Alex and gave her a big hug. "Thank you so much for teaching me how to chip the ball," Kat said. "It worked great!"

Alex smiled. "I only showed you the shot," she said. "You're the one who did it. Keep working on your skills like that and maybe you'll be able to play on the Breakers when you get older!"

A NEW PLAY

Later that day, the MVP Club ended up at Kat and Luke's house. They were hanging out on the back deck with Alex Akers. Kat's mom had put out a bunch of food. There was a big blue cooler filled with PowerPunch and another one filled with ice cream. Kat and Alice were still in their soccer uniforms. Everyone was sitting around the table celebrating the win.

"That was an amazing move, Kat," Alice said. "When we tied the game, I knew you would be the one to help us win. That's why we got something for you."

Alice dug inside her backpack and pulled out a shiny gold medal on a red, white, and blue ribbon.

"We decided you're our soccer MVP!"

Alice said. She hung the medal around Kat's neck.

Kat's face broke into a wide smile. "Thanks, everyone," she said. "Maybe someday this will be me." She pointed at the picture of Alex on the label of her drink.

"You know, Kat, being a soccer star isn't just about getting your picture on the PowerPunch bottle," Alex said. "It's also about working hard and believing in yourself, even when you mess up. *Especially* when you mess up. That's when it's most important to put your head down and just keep working. I'm proud of how hard you worked and the fact that you stuck with it. It was nice to see it pay off."

Kat smiled. "It felt great to have it pay off," she said. "Thanks for all your help."

Kat's mother brought out the model of the field house. She put it in the middle of the table. Then she put a hammer down next to it.

"What's that for?" Kat asked.

"To open it up!" her mother said. "How else are we going to get the money out?"

Kat smacked her head with her palm. "Mom! We're trying to *save* the field house, not destroy it!" she said. "Do you think I didn't leave a way to get the money out?"

Kat leaned over and stuck her fingernail into the side of the front door. The little door popped open. Dollar bills and coins tumbled out.

The table broke into laughter. Then Max and Nico started clapping. "Another great job, Kat!" Nico said.

For the next half hour, they counted the money. When they were done, they handed it over to Kat's mother.

"That's a lot of money," Kat's mom said. "It's amazing that we were able to raise so much in such a short time. But I have some bad news: I checked with the town planner, and I just don't think this will be enough to stop the town from selling the field house."

Kat sat up straight. "Oh no!" she said. "Isn't there anything else we can do?"

Kat's mom shrugged. "We'll try," she said. "But I don't know."

Nico and Luke moaned.

"I can't believe we worked so hard and we still failed," Max said.

"You didn't fail," Kat's mom said. "But sometimes even when you try, you're not always able to do what you want."

While Kat's mom put the money away, the kids sat around the table trying to figure out other ways to raise money. Alice suggested a dog-walking service. Nico thought of selling healthy snacks at school. Max just spun his chair around and tried to get something helpful to pop out of his brain.

But it looked like there'd be no way to save the field house.

A short time later, the doorbell rang. Kat's mom went to answer it. She seemed to be gone for a while. Finally, she returned. But she wasn't alone. Just behind her was Mr. Danforth!

He stood on the deck with his hands in his pockets. "Sorry to interrupt your party," he said. "But I had an idea and wanted to stop by."

Mr. Danforth looked at Kat and Alice. "What a terrific soccer game!" he said. "Kat, that was one of the most amazing moves I've ever seen on a soccer field."

Kat blushed. "Thank you," she said. She glanced at Alex. "I had a good teacher."

"I'll say," Mr. Danforth said. "But

I didn't come to talk soccer with you. I came over because I wanted to talk about the field house."

Mr. Danforth turned to Kat's mom. "Max, Nico, and Luke gave me a tour of it during the soccer game."

"We saw him exploring and wanted to make sure nothing went wrong," Luke said.

"You're not supposed to go in there," Kat's mom said to the kids. "I hope it was safe."

Mr. Danforth nodded. "It was," he said. "The boys really gave me some things to think about. That's how I came up with a new idea for the field house."

"What?" Luke and Kat asked together.

"I'm going to ask the town to let me buy it and fix it up," Mr. Danforth said.

"But that's what you were doing already," Max said.

Mr. Danforth smiled. "Actually, it isn't," he said. "After taking the tour of the field house with you today, I thought of something different."

Mr. Danforth pointed to Kat's field house model on the table.

"What if we share it?" Mr. Danforth asked. "I'll put my offices on the second floor. Then, with the money you raised today, we can turn the first floor into an activity center for the town. We can build out the snack bar and Alice's golf room."

"Really?" Max said. "That would be awesome!"

"Yes," said Mr. Danforth. "And I think we can even build a pretty neat rock-climbing wall on one side of the building!"

"Yeah!" Nico said. "I've always wanted to try rock climbing!"

"What a great idea," Kat's mom said. "You'll get your offices, and the town will get a great new activity center!"

The kids all clapped and hooted.

Mr. Danforth smiled. "I wouldn't have thought of it without the help of Max, Nico, and Luke," he said.

Max got up. "And I have another idea," he said. He went over to the cooler and opened the lid. He reached in and scooped out a big ball of blue raspberry ice cream and put it in one of the cones.

Max took the cone over to Mr. Dan-

forth. "One *cool* idea deserves another,"
he said. "To our new field house friend,
Mr. Danforth!"

The kids cheered for Mr. Danforth.
He raised his cone and took a bite.

"And when we get the field house
fixed up," he said. "I'll buy ice cream
for anyone who can beat me to the top
of the rock-climbing wall!"

Soccer

SOCCER POSITIONS. Soccer teams usually have one goalkeeper and ten field players. The team splits the field players into three kinds of positions: forwards, midfielders, and defenders.

⭐ A forward's job is to score goals.

⭐ Midfielders pass the ball up the field to the forwards, and they also try to help keep the ball away from their own goal.

⭐ Defenders play closest to their team's goal and must stop the other team from scoring.

A coach can organize the forwards, midfielders, and defenders into many different formations. Here's an example of one:

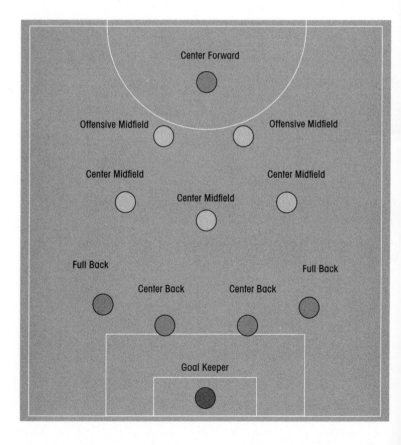

ANCIENT HISTORY. Sports that feature kicking leather balls into nets have been around for thousands of years. Modern soccer emerged in England in 1863, when teams met to create rules.

WHAT'S IT CALLED? Soccer is called soccer in the United States. But it's called football almost everywhere else in the world.

THE WORLD CUP. The World Cup is the biggest soccer tournament. Billions (yes, billions!) of people watch it. There is a tournament for men's teams and a tournament for women's teams. The women's World Cup typically takes place one year after the men's. Both are played every four years in a different country. The winner receives the World

Cup Trophy. The original men's trophy was stolen in 1983 and has never been found! The current trophy is fourteen inches tall and made of solid gold. It weighs over thirteen pounds!

RUNNING. Some soccer players run seven miles or more in a World Cup game.

ONE TOUGH GAME. As of July 2015, the biggest defeat in international soccer was Fiji's 38–0 win over Micronesia. The match was part of the 2015 Pacific Games. This tournament was an early step in qualifying for the 2016 Olympics.

TIME TO GO PRO? Recently, a twenty-month-old was signed to a professional soccer contract in Belgium. Although it's much too early to tell if young

Bryce Brites will be any good at soccer when he grows up, the soccer team (FC Racing Boxberg) thinks he's very good . . . for his age.

TRY THIS AT HOME. Dan Magness from England holds the world record for keeping a soccer ball in the air without dropping it or touching it with his hands. In 2010, Dan juggled a soccer ball using his feet, legs, chest, shoulders, and head for twenty-six hours!

NO SHOES, NO PLAYING. One of the reasons that India withdrew from the 1950 World Cup was because its team wasn't allowed to play barefoot!

FALLING DOWN. In a 1938 World Cup semifinal game, an Italian player's shorts fell down just before an important penalty kick! While the goalie was laughing at what had happened, Giuseppe Meazza quickly picked his shorts back up and made his shot. He scored! The goal got Italy into the World Cup final.

COOL MOVES!

Sometimes players do amazing kicks. They are one of the great things that make soccer such an exciting game to watch. Here are two examples of surprising kicks:

THE RAINBOW KICK. A rainbow kick is used to help a player get past a defender. To do a rainbow kick, you roll the ball up the back of your leg and then flick it up over your head. The ball will fly into the air over the top of your head, arcing like a rainbow, and land in front of you. (You can even make the ball go over the top of an opponent in front of you!)

1. Trap the ball between your feet. One foot is in front of the ball. The other foot is behind.

2. Use the top of your back foot to roll the ball up the calf of your front leg.

3. Lean forward and pop your heel up. This will flick the ball into the air.

THE BICYCLE KICK. Bicycle kicks are usually used to make a shot. They're also called scissor kicks. To do a bicycle kick, a player jumps up and falls back while the ball is in the air.

As the player falls back, they kick the ball over and behind them.

NOTE: Bicycle kicks can be dangerous!
Talk to a parent or coach before you try one.

Turn the page for a sneak peek at

"Blue twenty-two!" Nico yelled. "Hut, hut, hike!"

Nico snapped the football back to his friend Max. Their friends Alice and Luke counted five-Mississippi and sprang forward. They were trying to grab one of the blue flags hanging from either side of Max's waist before he could pass the ball or run by them.

"Come on, Max!" called Luke's sister, Kat, from the sideline.

Max tucked the ball under his arm and started to run. Alice headed straight for him. Max dodged to the left to get away. But as he did, the ball slipped through his fingers.

"Oh no! It's a fumble!" Kat yelled as the ball bounced end over end down the field. The flag football rules at Franklin Elementary School allowed fumbles, backward passes (or laterals), and a few other plays that made it more like regular football. Just no tackling!

Before Max could recover the football, Alice scooped it up. She tucked it under her arm and zipped down the field. There was no way for Nico or Max to catch up. Alice was a fast runner. A second later, she crossed the goal line.

Touchdown!

Nico's shoulders slumped. He brushed his dark hair back. Nico was one of the best athletes at Franklin Elementary School. He loved playing any kind of sports, but he didn't like losing. He held up his hands and shook them in pretend anger. "Max!" he said. "Not again!"

At the far end of the football field, Alice held the ball up and spiked it into the ground. She pointed at Max and smiled.

"Butterfingers!" she called. "Max has butterfingers!"

Max scuffed the field with his sneaker. "I'm just tired," he said. "We've been practicing forever!" Max liked reading more than sports. But he loved playing with his friends.

It was Wednesday afternoon. Max, Nico, Luke, Alice, Kat, and the rest of their team had spent an hour practicing football after school. They were getting ready for a big game against Hamilton Elementary School on Saturday.

But after practice had finished, the five friends decided to stay even later to work on a few more plays. Kat was the team's coach.

Kat ran onto the field from the sidelines. The purple ribbons she used to tie her curly hair back streamed along behind her. She waved her clipboard. "Alice, teasing Max isn't helping!" she yelled. "Everyone come here and huddle up."

Alice ran back as Max, Nico, and Luke huddled with Kat.

"Max, that was a good try, but you've got to hold on to the ball better, like this," Kat said. She took the ball from Alice and tucked it under her right arm. "Use your fingers to hold the front of the ball and press the back of it against your biceps. Then hold it tight against your chest. That will make it harder to drop. We can't make any mistakes if we want to beat Hamilton."

"The only way we're going to beat Hamilton is if they turn into eggs and someone gives us a whisk," Luke said. He loved to joke, but no one laughed. Luke looked around. "Didn't you get it?" he asked. "Eggs? Beat them?" Still, no one laughed. They were all too tired from practice. Luke shook his head. "It's your loss," he said. "You're missing a good *yolk*!"

Nico groaned. "Oh, that's bad," he said.

"But not as bad as our chance of beating Hamilton," Max said. "Maybe we can figure out a secret plan to win!" Max was big on secrets and special plans. He wanted to be a detective when he grew up, like his father. He had even gone to detective camp last summer.

Kat nodded. "We might need a secret weapon to win. Even with all our practicing, it doesn't look good. Hamilton has won five out of the last six years. It always seems like their players are bigger than us."

"But they're not!" Max said. "Well, they may be bigger than me, but they're in the same grade as us." Max was the smallest one of the group.

"But that's not what makes them better than us," Kat said. "They always beat us because they practice so much! They start practicing in the summer for this game. They always have special plays."

Nico clapped his hands together. "That's it! I've got it," he said. "I know how to win Saturday's game against Hamilton! This is a job for the MVP Club!"

Everybody turned to look at him. A little while ago, the five friends had helped save their school Olympics by discovering who was trying to sabotage the games. They were awarded Most Valuable Player medals. After that, the kids had decided to form the MVP Club to play sports and have adventures together.

"How can the MVP Club beat Hamilton?" Alice asked.

"It's easy," Nico said. "All we have to do is spy on Hamilton's practice tomorrow after school and learn their plays!"

"Pssst! Kat!" Max whispered. "Keep your head down!"

Kat ducked. The blue butterfly clips in her hair bounced. It was Thursday afternoon, and she and Max were hiding behind a brick wall outside Hamilton Elementary School. The rest of the MVP Club had decided to stay behind.

"Follow me," Max whispered. "But stay down so we don't get caught! If the Hamilton team knows we're here, they might beat us up or something!"

He led Kat along the wall that ringed the athletic field behind the school. The Hamilton football team had just come out to practice.

Max and Kat crept along the wall toward the bleachers on the far side of the field.

They could hear the calls of Hamilton's quarterback.

"Red twenty-four! Red twenty-four! Hut, hut, hike!"

Max and Kat peeked over the top of the wall to watch the action. The Hamilton team wore matching football jerseys. The players on offense wore red. The players on defense wore white. They also had matching football shoes with plastic cleats. They looked a lot more professional than the Franklin team.

The Hamilton quarterback was so large, he looked like a middle school kid. Two receivers had run far down the field as their defense tried to stop them. The players around the quarterback blocked the rushers so he had time to make a throw. Two seconds later, he saw an opening and let the football fly. It sailed high into the sky and came down right before the end zone. The Hamilton receiver shot to his right and held his arms out. The football dropped into his hands like someone had placed it there. One more step and he was across the line.

Touchdown!

Kat let out a whistle. "Wow!" she whispered. "They look like an NFL team compared to us!"

Max sank down on his heels. "I know," he said. "That's why we need to find a way to win. Otherwise, we won't have a chance."

Kat tugged his shirt. "Come on," she said. "Once we get to our hiding spot, we can study their plays."

They continued along the outside wall until there was an opening. A few minutes later, Max and Kat had found their way under the shiny silver bleachers. It was dark and damp, but they had a clear view of the field from between the rows of seats.

"This is great!" Kat said. "It's so easy to spy on their practice!"

Max nodded. He pulled a pen and small notebook out of his back pocket. "You watch and tell me what they're doing, and I'll write it down," he said.

For the next half an hour, Kat and Max studied the Hamilton team. They watched as the team ran through one play after the other. Kat would describe the plays, and Max would write them down. Kat also used her phone to take pictures.

Hamilton's quarterback looked good.

But one of the other Hamilton players really stuck out. His name was Logan. He was taller and bigger than most of the other players. Even though the quarterback called the plays, Logan kept telling the other players what to do.

"I can't believe you just dropped that pass!" he yelled at one. "We're not going to win with mistakes like that!"

A few plays later, Logan exploded when one of the smaller Hamilton players didn't run fast enough. "My grandmother runs faster than that!" Logan hollered. "You're out for the next five plays."

The player went and sat on the sidelines while another one took his place.

"Wow, Logan's hard on his teammates," Max said. "That kid *was* running fast."

Kat nodded. "Yeah, he likes picking on people," she said. "It's too bad because Logan actually seems to be a pretty good player."

Hamilton kept practicing. And Logan kept yelling at different teammates. When a player flubbed a handoff, Logan got three other kids to tease him. The three kept dropping the football and pretending to cry. Logan laughed out loud. But it looked like the player who had made the mistake was the one who really wanted to cry.

Shortly after, the football team took a break for water. Max looked over his notes. He had written down a bunch of Hamilton's plays and formations and taken notes on the different players.

"They're a really good team, even if Logan's mean," Kat said.

Max nodded. "They are definitely better than us," he said.

He looked at the notebook in his hands. He thought for a moment, and then his eyes lit up.

"But we're a good team, too," he said. "And more importantly, they're not perfect! They make mistakes just like us. And Logan's big, but he's a bully. I think we can win!"

Max tapped the notebook against the back of his hand. Then he threw the notebook into the dirt. "What did you do that for?" Kat asked. She leaned over and picked it up.

"You know, we *are* a good team. Too good to be doing this," Max said. "We need to win because we did our best. Not because we spied and cheated."

Kat looked at Max for a moment. Then she nodded. "Yeah, you're right," she said. "This seemed like a good idea, but we're better than this. Let's rip up the notes and leave!"

Max took the notebook back. Then he pulled out the pages he had written on and tore them all up. He tossed them into a nearby trash can.

"Let's get out of here," he said.

Kat nodded. They slipped out from under the bleachers and tried to sneak around to the other side of the brick wall.

"Hey, stop them!" called out one of the Hamilton players. Max and Kat froze. They'd been spotted! "They've been spying on our practice!"

The players on the Hamilton team started to run for Max and Kat!

"Quick!" Kat said. They scrambled around the brick wall and ran for their bikes.

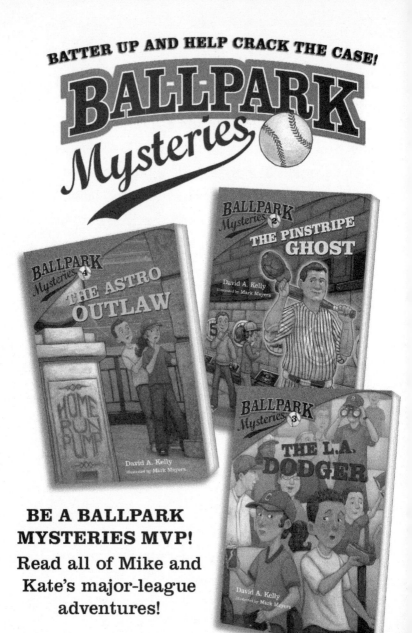